Lucille Clifton

EVERETT ANDERSON'S FRIEND

illustrations by
Ann Grifalconi

HOUGHTON MIFFLIN COMPANY BOSTON

Atlanta   Dallas   Geneva, Illinois   Palo Alto   Princeton   Toronto

Houghton Mifflin Edition, 1993

Printed in the U.S.A.

ISBN 0-395-61770-7

456789-B-96 95 94 93

To Everett Anderson's Friends   L.C.

To the Friends We Keep   A.G.

Someone new has come to stay
in 13A, in 13A
and Everett Anderson's Mama and he
can't wait to see, can't wait to see
whether it's girls or
whether it's boys and
how are their books and
how are their toys and
where they've been and
where they go and
who are their friends and
the people they know,
oh, someone new has come to stay
next door in 13A.

If not an almost
brother,
why not something
other
like a bird or
a cat or
a cousin or
a dozen uncles?

Please,
says Everett Anderson softly,
why did they have to be
a family of
shes?

Girls named Maria who
win at ball
are not a bit of fun
at all.
No, girls who can run
are just no fun
thinks Everett Anderson!

In 14A when Mama's at work
sometimes Joe and sometimes Kirk
can come till she gets home and be
Everett Anderson's company.

Three boys are just the right amount
for playing games that count,
there isn't any room, you see,
for girls named Maria in company.

11

If Daddy was here
he would let me in and
call me a careless boy
and then
(even though I
  forgot my key)
he would make peanut butter
and jelly for me,
and not be mad
and I'd be glad.

If Daddy was here
he could let me in
thinks Everett Anderson
again.

A girl named Maria
is good to know
when you haven't got
any place to go
and you forgot your
apartment key.

Why, she can say,
"Come in with me,
  and play in 13A and wait
  if your Mama is working late."

Even if she beats at races it's
nicer to lose in familiar places.

Maria's Mama makes little pies
called *Tacos,*
calls little boys *Muchachos,*
and likes to thank the *Dios;*
oh, 13A is a lovely surprise
to Everett Anderson's eyes!

Everett Anderson's Mama is mad
because he lost the key he had;
but a boy has so many things to do
he can't remember them and keys, too.
And if Daddy were here he would say,
"We'll talk about it another day,"
thinks the boy who got a fussing at
for just a little thing like that.

A girl named Maria
who wins at ball
is fun to play with
after all
and Joe and Kirk and
Maria too
are just the right number
for things to do.

Lose a key,
win a friend,
things have a way of
balancing out,
Everett Anderson's Mama explains,
and that's what the world is all about.

And the friends we find
are full of surprises
Everett Anderson realizes.

ABOUT THE AUTHOR

Lucille Clifton is an award-winning poet and the author of *Some of the Days of Everett Anderson, Everett Anderson's Christmas Coming, All Us Come Cross the Water, The Times They Used to Be, Everett Anderson's Year,* and of *My Brother Fine With Me.* She and her husband live with their six children in Baltimore, Maryland.

ABOUT THE ARTIST

Ann Grifalconi, a native New Yorker, has written and illustrated several books, including the ever-popular *The Toy Trumpet.* As an illustrator, she has collaborated with many writers on over thirty books, including *Everett Anderson's Year.*

ABOUT THE BOOK

The art for this book was done in pen and ink on rice paper.
The type faces used were Times Roman, Windsor Outline, and Avant Garde.